To Emma—
It's a perfect
day to read! ☺
Shannon
Anderson

Penelope Perfect

A Tale of Perfectionism Gone Wild

Shannon Anderson

Illustrated by
Katie Kath

free spirit
PUBLISHING®

Library of Congress Cataloging-in-Publication Data

Anderson, Shannon, 1972–
    Penelope perfect : a tale of perfectionism gone wild / Shannon Anderson ; illustrated by Katie Kath.
        pages cm
    ISBN 978-1-63198-019-0 (hardback) — ISBN 978-1-63198-047-3 (softcover) 1. Perfectionism (Personality trait)—Juvenile literature.
I. Kath, Katie, illustrator. II. Title.
    BF698.35.P47A53 2015
    155.4'18232—dc23

2015008984

Free Spirit Publishing does not have control over or assume responsibility for author or third-party websites and their content.

Reading Level Grade 2; Interest Level Ages 5–9;
Fountas & Pinnell Guided Reading Level K

Illustrations by Katie Kath
Edited by Alison Behnke
Cover and interior design by Michelle Lee Lagerroos

10 9 8 7 6 5 4 3 2 1
Printed in China
R18860615

Free Spirit Publishing Inc.
217 Fifth Avenue North, Suite 200
Minneapolis, MN 55401-1299
(612) 338-2068
help4kids@freespirit.com
www.freespirit.com

Free Spirit offers competitive pricing.
Contact edsales@freespirit.com for pricing information on multiple quantity purchases.

This book is dedicated
to my sisters,
Tara and Ashley,
who each have a bit of
Penelope in them.

They call me Penelope Perfect.
If you know me, I'm sure you agree.

Have you ever heard of Old Faithful?
Well, that geyser has *nothin'* on me!

OLD FAITHFUL GEYSER
12
3
6
9
ERUPTS ON SCHEDULE EVERY DAY!
"A sight to see!"
YELLOWSTONE NATIONAL PARK

I wake up at five every morning
To begin my daily routine.

I smooth all the wrinkles out of my sheets,
And make my room perfectly clean.

Next, I do 10 jumping jacks
To follow my exercise chart.

For breakfast, I always eat pancakes.
My mom makes them shaped like a heart!

I pack up my lunchbox and schoolbag.
I get dressed and I feed my cat, Gus.

I kiss my mom and dad good-bye,
And head outside to the bus.

7

At school I straighten my desk, just so.
I sharpen six pencils, too.

I ask about extra credit
And recheck the work that is due.

At lunchtime I pull out some wet wipes
To kill all the germs on the table.

I turn all my food to face me
So I can read every label.

At recess I rewrite my lessons.
(I can't *stand* to have sloppy notes!)

I practice my spelling words twice,
And brush up on my Abe Lincoln quotes.

I climb on the bus to go home,
And tackle my schoolwork at four.

I eat dinner with Mom and Dad,
Then study my lessons some more.

I put on my favorite pj's,
Brush my teeth and comb my hair.

My parents tuck me in at eight
With my cat and my teddy bear.

I don't fall asleep till much later.
There are so many thoughts in my head.

I need to double-check the list
I keep safely by my bed.

I love to be prepared,
With every detail on track.

But sometimes a sudden storm
Throws things way out of whack.

I snooze through the thunder and lightning,
Deep in a *very* sound sleep.

And at five o'clock in the morning,
My trusty alarm doesn't beep.

The storm must have knocked out the power.
We've all slept till past eight o'clock!

I don't have time to shower,
Or even to find matching socks.

My bed is rumpled!
My hair is a mess!

I can't fix the wrinkles
In my polka-dot dress.

I run to my parents' room,
Crying, "What are we going to do?

My watch says it's 8:17—
Please tell me it isn't true!"

My dad leaps straight out of bed
While I scoop up all my stuff.

The plum I grab for breakfast
Will have to be enough.

Dad takes me to school, and I gulp.
What will the other kids say?

I've never been late for anything.
I just *know* this will be a bad day.

The tardy bell rings through the hallway.
I sigh and open the door.

Everyone turns as I walk in the room,
And their jaws nearly hit the floor.

With my unbraided hair and wrinkled dress,
My mismatched shoes and sweater,

I look like I've been through a hurricane!
I sure hope my day will get better.

I wonder what I'll eat for lunch today,
Since I didn't have time to pack it.

And what if my pencils all break in two?
I'm not sure I can hack it.

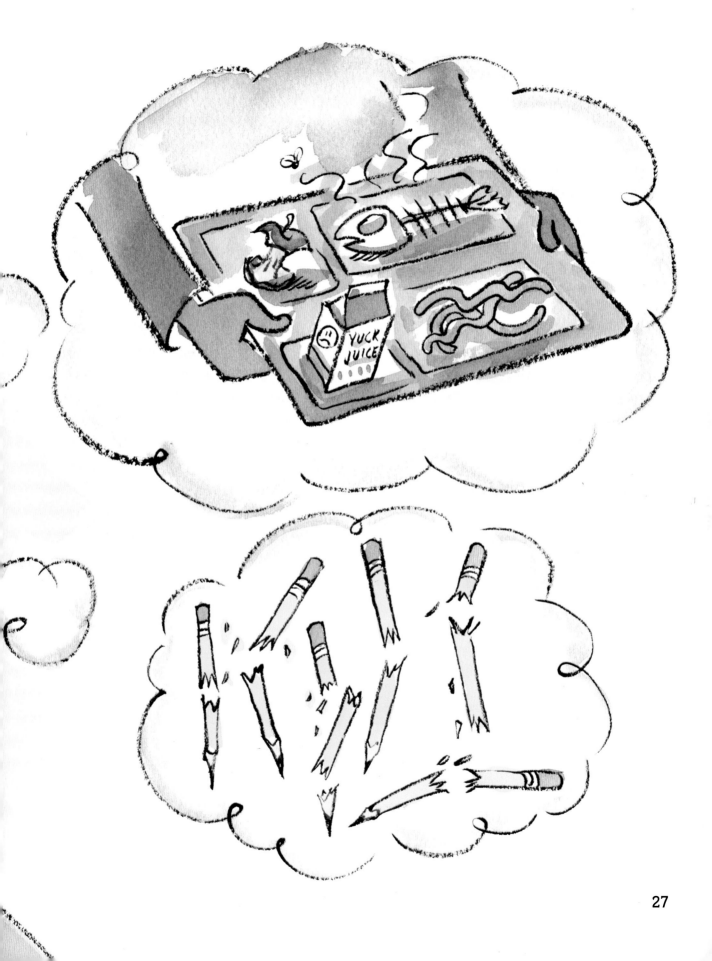

Just when I think things can't get worse,
I get my first-ever "B."

I slump in my chair with my head on the desk.
What a catastrophe!

My teacher walks over to see me.
I'm sure she senses disaster.

I kind of feel like crying . . .
But instead, I burst into laughter.

Why do I feel so giddy?
Something strange is happening to me.

My wrinkled clothes are so comfy,
And my messy hair makes me feel free!

I decide to go out for recess.
My notes can wait for a while.

The other kids look surprised at first—
And then they start to smile.

To think of all those days I stayed in,
When I could have been playing kickball.

The truth is, I can't stop smiling.
Recess is fun, after all!

A wonderful feeling of freedom
Fills up my mind and my heart.

Maybe a day *can* end happy,
Even after a terrible start.

I survive this memorable school day,
Do my homework, and help Mom and Dad.

I even leave time to play outside.
I guess goofing off isn't so bad!

I've learned not to make life a checklist.
That doesn't mean that I'm lazy.

It's all right to go with the flow sometimes,
And not make myself so crazy.

I've decided that from now on
I won't be in such a big hurry.

I'll still try my best in all I do,
But I'll try *not* to constantly worry.

They called me Penelope Perfect.
That was once who I wanted to be.

But now I think it's better
To just be Penelope.

Activities and Discussion Questions

Penelope's story can be a jumping-off place for conversation, reflection, and fun with children in school settings, at home, or elsewhere. The following activities and questions offer some ideas to get started. Feel free to adapt them and add your own.

Laugh Out Loud

Invite children to talk about how being able to laugh when things don't go according to plan can help them face challenges and cope with unexpected situations.

After your discussion, split children up into smaller groups of three or four and have each group create a short, funny skit about a day that goes all wrong. Encourage children to exaggerate and get really silly. Then have groups perform their skits.

Learning and Growing

Making mistakes is a natural part of life, especially as we learn and grow. As a group, talk about examples of this concept. If children need help getting started, suggest some ideas, such as a toddler learning to walk, a kid learning to ride a bike, or a basketball player practicing layups. You might also share stories of famous people who experienced failure before they became successful, such as Dr. Seuss, J.K. Rowling, or Michael Jordan. Ask questions such as:

- What do you think people can learn from their mistakes? How can they use that knowledge later on?

- What is a time when you made a mistake? What did you do about it? Do you feel different about it now than you did at the time? How so?

- What is something you'd like to learn to do? How can you handle the challenges and mistakes that go along with learning something new?

What If?

Children can sometimes get stressed by minor details and obsess about the ways things might go wrong. Propose some hypothetical situations to your group and ask them to brainstorm things that *could* happen as a result of each. Try to make these scenarios realistic, but not too serious. For example, what if:

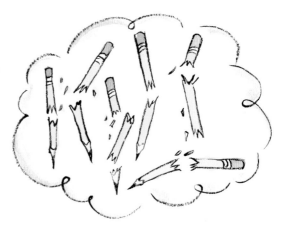

- Joseph forgets a school book at home?
- Mikaela's cat knocks over a glass of water and it spills all over her homework?
- Adnan's little brother moved his stuff around, and now Adnan can't find a toy he borrowed from a friend?
- Bai is setting the table when she drops a glass and it breaks?

Talk about children's ideas, their possible implications, and how likely they are to happen. Help children see that worries can grow larger than life sometimes. If you like, have the group role-play these scenarios and how children might cope with them.

Hop to It

Invite children to work together (in one large group, or in small groups) to draw a hopscotch outline on mural paper, or outdoors on a blacktop or other surface. Ask children to choose a goal or a desire and draw it in the highest-numbered space. Then have them decorate each remaining space of the outline with drawings of things that they like and things that are fun to do. Some of these drawings can be related to the goal, but they don't have to be.

Remind children that each day brings many possibilities and many ways to get to the same outcome or goal, that sometimes goals change, and that even when we don't reach our goals, we might discover new friends, interests, and adventures along the way.

Then, especially if you're outside, play!

Explore the Story

Discuss the story of Penelope and her topsy-turvy day.
Refer back to particular pages of the book as needed, and
ask children questions such as the following:

- Where do you think the nickname "Penelope Perfect" came from?
  How do you think Penelope feels about her nickname?

- Why do you think Penelope's routine and schedule are so important
  to her? Do you like to do some things the same way every day, or do you like to
  mix it up? Why or why not?

- How do you think Penelope feels about the idea of making mistakes? How do *you*
  feel about making mistakes? How do you respond when you do make a mistake?

- Why doesn't Penelope go to sleep right away the night of the big thunderstorm?
  What kinds of thoughts do you think are going through her mind?

A Note to Caring Adults

As a perfectionist myself, I know how draining the pressure to succeed can be.
Whether that pressure comes from others or is self-imposed, the feeling that
you need everything to go a certain way is very real. It's easy to assume you've
failed when plans don't work out the way you hope. And even when you logically
understand that you can't get everything exactly right every time, the feeling that
you've disappointed yourself or others is uncomfortable.

When Penelope's alarm doesn't go off and her normal routine is thrown out of
whack, she feels like she isn't in control. She worries that she will not look her best,
do her best at school, or be prepared to handle unexpected situations. She has to
face what happens if she arrives late, has messy hair, or dares to give herself time
to go out and enjoy recess. Through this process, Penelope discovers that Earth
doesn't fall off its axis and she makes it through the day safely. To her surprise, she
even has some fun!

There are many ways you can help children like Penelope reach similar
understandings. For example, you can model resilience and positive thinking
when *you* make mistakes. You can guide children to set realistic expectations
and attainable goals that also stretch their abilities and comfort zones. You can
encourage students by praising their efforts, rather than their intelligence. For
instance, when a child earns an A on a paper or wins a spelling bee, you could
say, "Wow! You must have really worked hard!" rather than, "You are so smart!"
Similarly, when providing praise, focus on the process rather than the product.
This encourages students to take healthy risks and try new things.

Above all, you can do what you already do: support, nurture, and listen to
children. And enjoy the journey! My best wishes go with you.

—Shannon Anderson

- Why do you think Penelope is so worried about having messy hair and a wrinkled dress? Did anything bad happen as a result of her hair and clothes? Have you ever been worried about something that didn't turn out to be a big deal? How can you deal with worries like that?

- Why do you think Penelope is anxious about what might happen as the day goes on? When you have to deal with new situations, how do you feel? What are some times when a new situation ended up being really fun?

- When the other students get over the surprise of Penelope joining them for recess, how do they react? How do you think it feels for her to play with her friends at recess? What are some of your favorite ways to play?

- How do you think Penelope feels at the end of the day after the storm? How does that compare to how she felt at the beginning? When is a time that you expected something to go one way, and it went another? What did you learn from that experience?

- What do you think Penelope means when she says, "Now I think it's better to just be Penelope"? What does it mean to be yourself? What are some things you like about being you?

A Psychologist's Perspective

Perfectionism is a mindset that narrows a person's ability to see or imagine a range of possibilities. That means a child who has perfectionistic traits sees only one "right" outcome, rather than several valid ways to complete a task. Any misstep along the way can become a reason to harshly blame herself (or himself) or others for perceived failures. Perfectionism generally takes two main forms: a child expects herself to be perfect, and she believes that others expect her to be perfect. The more a child feels she must perform without fault, the more likely she is to experience sadness, guilt, anxiety, and in some cases, social stress and angry behaviors as well.

While not every perfectionist will experience the same difficulties, perfectionism *can* take a toll on a child's health and happiness. That's why it's important for caring adults to help children work through perfectionistic tendencies and build new patterns of thinking and behaving. If you see signs of perfectionism in a child, help her understand that while routine and order can be comforting, being able to adapt is a powerful skill. Reinforce the fact that excellence and high standards are not the same as perfection. Communicate the ideas that challenges can be energizing and fun, and mistakes are part of life—for everyone! Support the child in the adventure of trying new things. Most of all, model good humor. Be willing to share times when you struggled and perhaps failed, along with what you learned from those experiences. Through these strategies, you can help children be healthier, happier, and more successful.

—*Chad Pulver, Ph.D.*

About the Author and Illustrator

Shannon Anderson remembers having a very neat bedroom when she was young, much like Penelope's. In fact, she used to reorganize it on the weekends just for fun. After having kids (and many pets), she has learned how to let some things go and be okay with having her house look less than perfect! Shannon is a literacy coach, high ability coordinator, adjunct professor, and children's book author. She was born and raised in Indiana and lives there with her husband, Matt, and their two daughters, Emily and Madison—plus a dog, two cats, a turtle, and two snails. Her favorite things include spending time with her family, writing, teaching, running, and eating ice cream. Shannon also enjoys doing author visits at schools and events. You can find out more about her at www.shannonisteaching.com.

Katie Kath is an international award-winning freelance illustrator who creates book and magazine artwork for children of all ages, as well as for young adults. She currently lives in the rolling hills of North Carolina with her husband and their cat, and she tries not to be a perfectionist—sometimes.

Interested in purchasing multiple quantities and receiving volume discounts?
Contact edsales@freespirit.com or call 1.800.735.7323 and ask for Education Sales.

Many Free Spirit authors are available for speaking engagements, workshops, and keynotes.
Contact speakers@freespirit.com or call 1.800.735.7323.

For pricing information, to place an order, or to request a free catalog, contact:

free spirit PUBLISHING®

**217 Fifth Avenue North • Suite 200 • Minneapolis, MN 55401-1299 • toll-free 800.735.7323 • local 612.338.2068
fax 612.337.5050 • help4kids@freespirit.com • www.freespirit.com**